School

Come in and take a closer look

Britta Teckentrup

School
Come in and take a closer look

Translated by
Shelley Tanaka

PRESTEL
Munich · London · New York

I'm in sixth grade. I'll bet my school is like most others. Not good, not bad... just somewhere in between. Of course, there are lots of things that could be better, if anyone bothered to look around. A school is only as good as its teachers and students, its principal, your friends and parents...

A school is as diverse as its students. The more variety the better, I say. But it's not that easy for so many people to get along. It takes an open mind. Things can work out, though—if you have teachers who make learning fun, if you make real friends, if you feel like you matter. But you can't choose your teachers or your classmates, who don't always cooperate. That's when you get people competing for power, sucking up, trying to get attention. That's when you notice the differences between the strong and the weak, the brave and the scared, the quiet and the loud.

That's when people become outsiders just because they're different from others.

But what does being "different" really mean, and who gets to decide?

Come with me, and I'll show you how things work at our school...

The teachers are always talking about the

"school community," and the "classroom community."

But what exactly is community?

Does it mean that everyone has to be the same?

Wouldn't it be good if everyone could just be themselves,

without having to do what everybody else does?

Wouldn't it be braver and more interesting

if everyone could find their own way?

If everyone thinks and does the same thing,

then nothing can ever change.

Everyone in my school has
their own personal story.
I'll tell you about
a few of them...

This is Paul's first day. He's switched schools and hopes things will be better here than at his old school. That's where Fred goes, the kid who made life hard for him. At his old school no one helped Paul, so he's kind of nervous and hopes he'll find a friend here…

This morning Max is sitting in the schoolyard too.

He always waits until all the other kids are inside

the building before he goes in.

This means that sometimes he's almost late for class.

Why does he always want to go in last?

He has a good reason.

He doesn't want to run into Tom...

Tom told everyone not to hang
around with Max anymore.
I'm a bit scared of Tom too.
Even though he's not that
big or strong.

But Tom has a gang.

He's the leader, so his gang does what he says.

Tom is proud of his gang.

They make him feel strong.

Tom is really clever,

and the teachers believe everything he says...

No one likes him,

but everyone is scared of him.

Lisa's the only one who doesn't care. Tom can't do anything to her!

She's the only one who sometimes comforts Max.

Mr. Solis says, "Toughen up, Max!

Tom is actually a very nice boy.

You need to grow a thicker skin.

You're overreacting... you're just too sensitive.

It's your own fault if you let things like this

happen to you."

Sometimes this makes Max really furious,
but mostly it just makes him sad.
When he gets furious, he feels like fighting
and being as mean as Tom.
But Lisa says, "Don't be like him!"
Max hasn't trusted the teachers for a long time.
Sometimes Lisa is the only one he'll talk to.

If only he knew there were others who felt exactly the same way!
But why doesn't anyone dare tell him that?

It's her own fault that she's being bullied.

You have to ignore it.

Don't listen to them...

That's just the way kids are.

You'll have to sort it out for yourselves.

They're just kidding. Don't take it so seriously!

You'll have to grow a thicker skin.

They're just testing you.

It was the same when we were young.

It will all pass eventually...

It was just done in fun.

He didn't mean it!

You haven't always been an angel yourself.

Oh, don't be like that.

It wasn't as bad as all that.

That's the way girls are.

Just stay out of his way!

You'll never
amount to anything.

Lisa doesn't let anyone say stuff about her at school,

and she's not afraid of anything.

She's strong!

I'd like to be just like her.

But she doesn't talk about herself much,

and she's never invited anyone to her house.

She doesn't celebrate her birthday, either.

Everyone likes her, but she doesn't have a best friend.

Sometimes Lisa doesn't come to school.

I don't know why.

She says she had a stomachache...

"Can other people tell how I feel just by looking at me?"

Linda may not get the best marks, but she has the most beautiful voice I've ever heard! Sometimes it's more important to have a big passion and talent for something.

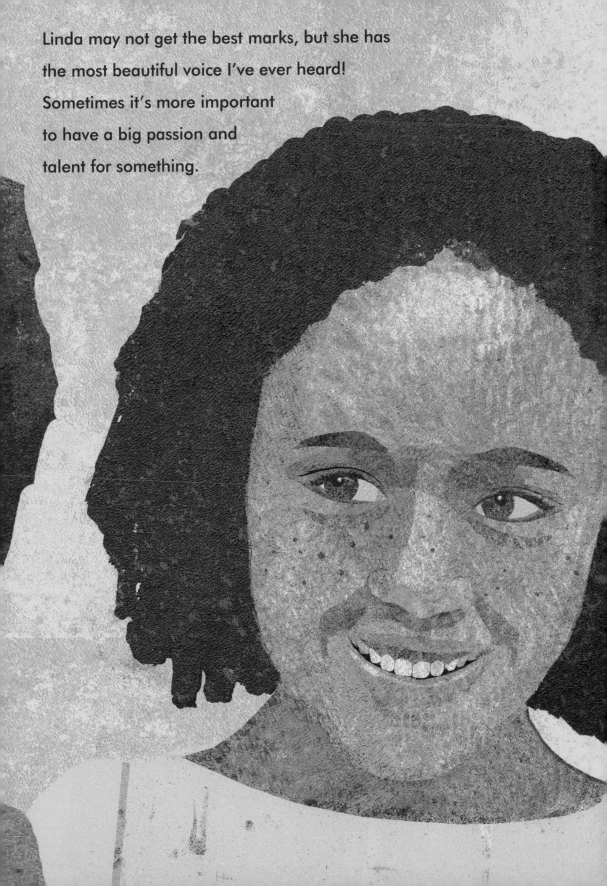

When she starts to sing,

everyone stops to listen.

"When I sing, I can forget about everything that's going on around me," Linda says.

For math and music, Linda has Ms. Akhter,
who saw how talented she was right away.

Ms. Akhter makes learning fun.

Ms. Akhter is Kathrin's math teacher too.
If Kathrin doesn't get at least a C
on her next math assignment,
she won't pass…

"We can do it! I'll help you.
You're a smart girl!"

I think good teachers are the ones who like their students.
When that happens, we like them back.

What will happen to all of us when we finish school,

and what if I don't pass?

What does it mean to be "successful"?

Does being successful make you happy forever?

Does it always mean having a job and money?

Why is it so important to get good marks all the time?

Jamila hasn't been at our school for long.

She comes from another country that's really far from here.

I like listening to her. She's got so many stories to tell,

and lots of them are sad. She had to escape from

her own country because there was a war there.

Everything is new and different for her here,

but she's always so positive. I hope things stay like that,

so she can follow her own path.

Jamila likes going to our school.

She works hard—twice as hard as anyone else.

She really brings a lot to our classroom community!

"When I grow up, I want to change the world," Jamila says.

"My history teacher, Mr. Davis, really believes in me. He says I can do it!

Most people don't think I can. We can't change things anyway.

And for sure you can't, they say. But I'm going to show them!"

"Are we really so different?"

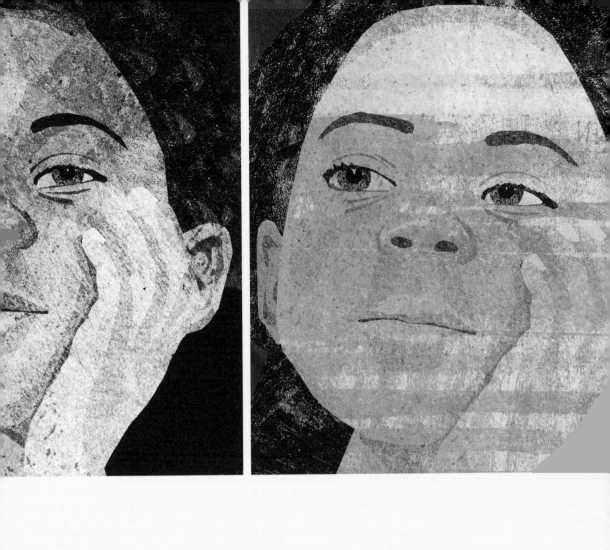

Talia is Paula's best friend.

They're always together.

They sit next to each other.

And whenever things aren't going so great
for Talia, Paula is there for her.
They are truly best friends.

Others are just plain mean
to one another.

Yesterday they locked Peter up in the closet again.

"When I was still little, I could shut my eyes really tight and then I wasn't even there. I wish things still worked that way. Then I could imagine myself someplace really far away..."

There's a lot of competition in gym,
where working together can quickly turn
into working against one another.

For example, there's Laura.

She hates sports!

And there's a reason for that...

Today in gym class, Sandy and Clara get to choose the teams, as usual. They're both really sporty.

They pick their friends first. Then they pick the athletic kids, to make sure their team will win.

Laura's the last to be picked, again.

"Will they pick me last again?"

Why does it matter if you
get picked first or last?

What does it really mean
to be a "winner" or "loser"?

Why does Mr. Peters let kids pick the teams in the first place?
He could do it and make the sides fair.
Is he just too lazy to do it himself?

Should you really give someone an F in gym?

Swimming lessons start soon...
Marie is kind of worried about it.

Today everyone has to dive down to the bottom of the deep end. You have to fetch a ring to get your swimming badge.

Last week, at practice, Marie couldn't do it.

Now she's worried that the same thing will happen today.

She's a good swimmer, but diving isn't her thing.

"Why do we have to get a silly badge in the first place?

And why isn't there a badge for trying, which takes at least

as much courage? Isn't the main thing to be a good swimmer?

And I am!"

But the others reassure her.

"You can do it, Marie. And if not, it's not
the end of the world!"

"We'll dive beside you, to make sure you're okay,"
say Fred and Milo.
"But you have to grab the ring yourself…"

Marie trusts them.
She gathers all her courage, gets in the water
and lets the ring sink to the bottom...

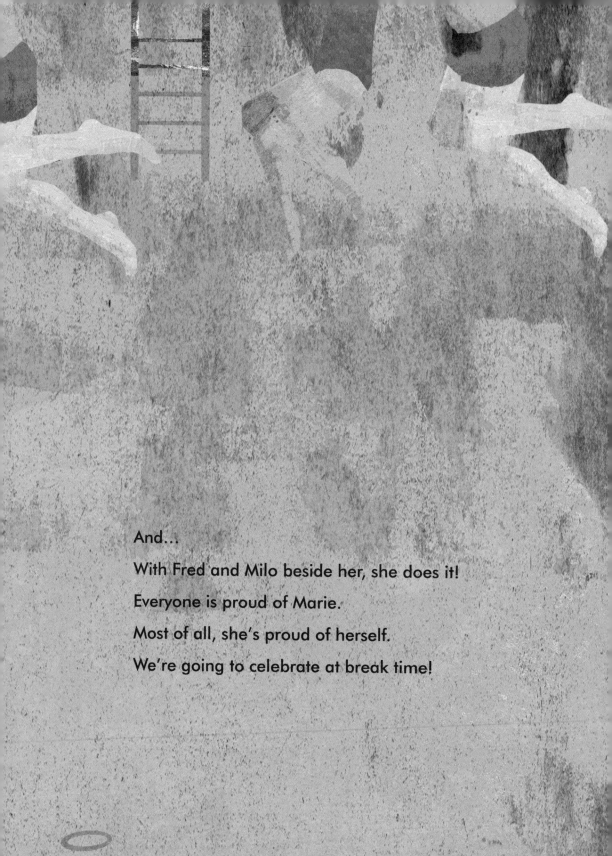

And…

With Fred and Milo beside her, she does it!

Everyone is proud of Marie.

Most of all, she's proud of herself.

We're going to celebrate at break time!

During break, they beat up on Max again.

And again, no one says anything.

Tim saw the whole thing. He feels so bad for Max.

But then, what should he do?

It would be just him against all of them,

and he doesn't want to end up in Max's shoes.

"Don't be a snitch!" the others tell him.

"You know what happens to rats.

Besides, no one's going to believe you anyway!"

What will Tim do?

Tim told his older sister all about it.

For Lisette there's just one solution.

"We have to tell the teachers,

so that it stops once and for all."

The thing with Tom and Max has now come to the attention of the principal. "There is no bullying in our school," he says. But he phones Tom's father.

But there is bullying!

Just listen to what they say in our school.

Go back where you came from!

You'll never amount to anything.

Start by learning to speak our language!

What's *he* doing here?

Go home then, if you don't have any friends!

You loser!

Learn how to read and write properly first!

You're just adopted…

He's crying like a girl.

If you don't want to be my best friend anymore,
then I'll make sure you have no friends at all.

Drop dead!

Who did you say you were, again?

You can't do it anyway!

Snitch!

But with luck, there's another side to things:

It's not your fault.

I believe you.   I'm listening.

What can we do about it together?

You're the stronger one.

I have time for you right now.

You're not the only one who feels this way, but everyone's afraid to speak up.

You're not alone.

Yes, I'm taking you seriously.

Come straight to me if that happens again.

You're stronger than you think!

I'll help you...

You're fantastic just the way you are.

In the afternoon, Tom's father came in
to see the teacher.

"That was definitely not my son! Tom would
never do such a thing. He's a good kid.
I don't want to say anything, but there seems
to be a lot going on with Max's family. Aren't
the parents separated? I don't like to judge…
maybe the mother is under some pressure?
Is Max as good a student as Tom?
You know, Tom wants to become a lawyer
one day, follow in my footsteps…
You have to consider both sides of the matter.
It always takes two…"

There's always a bit of teasing involved!

Boys will be boys.

Well, a bit of shoving is perfectly normal, isn't it?

And where is Max now?

No one has seen him since the break.

The school day just goes on as usual for most.

A lot of people probably don't even know what happened…

I run into Jackson in the hall. He's on his way to art class.

He'd rather not go, because that's where *she* is waiting.

He won't even say her name.

Her real name is Mrs. Cabot, but Jackson never calls her that.

He just calls her the Witch.

Can you be good in a subject that's not fun anymore?

You just picked art because you're no good at anything else!

Is math more important than art?

You can't tell she's a witch by looking at her. But Jackson knows she is one. Art was always his favourite subject and he just loved it—until the witch came.

"Art is a serious subject," she says. "In my class you need to work as hard as you do at math or science."

For the first art project he did in her class, Jackson got an F. An F! Just like that… from an A to an F! She told him he had to participate more, and that he couldn't paint at home because she wouldn't know if he had really done the work himself. She also couldn't help him if he painted at home. But Jackson loves to draw for himself, in his room…

Now he's lost all his enthusiasm, and he just sits in his place and scratches away. Mrs. Cabot never comes over to him. Besides, she'd really rather teach girls.

Can a teacher make you stop loving your favourite subject?

Should a teacher have favourite students?

Do some teachers prefer girls to boys?

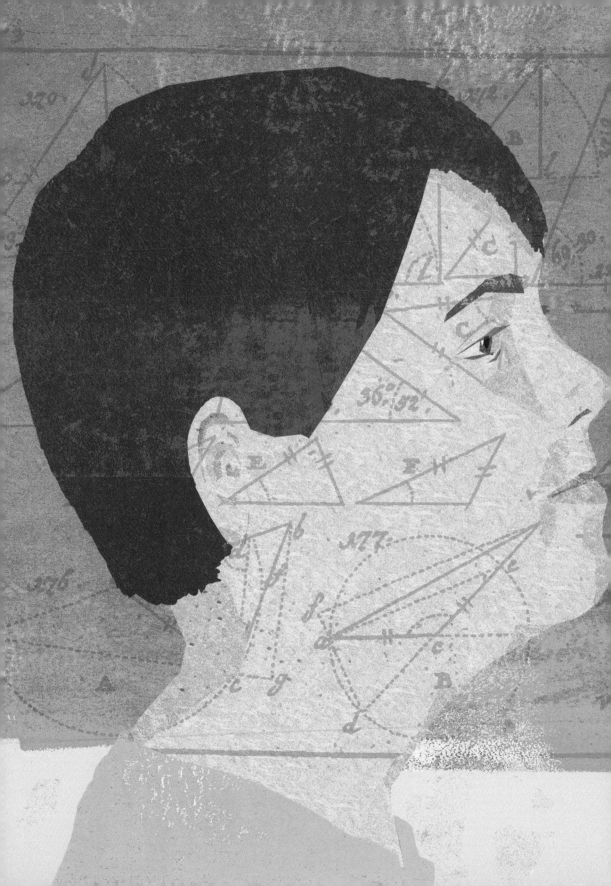

Dan doesn't care what Mrs. Cabot does.

He just lives in his own world and does things

his own way. He's a bit of a loner, and he

comes up with solutions that nobody else has

thought of. Even though he's got a weird way

about him, he's actually very smart. He always

says exactly what he thinks right away, without

worrying about what the others might feel.

I know he doesn't say things to be mean,

but sometimes he hurts people's feelings.

He really likes Marlene, but she doesn't want

to have anything to do with him.

As for Marlene...

What is beauty, and who decides what's beautiful?

Do beautiful people have an easier time of it?

Would I be just as popular if I weren't so beautiful?

Everyone thinks she's awesome!

She's absolutely gorgeous. But she can also be kind of stuck up. She just loves that everyone adores her, and she always looks so perfect.

She doesn't have to work at being popular, and she's always the centre of attention. But I think she finds it a bit exhausting, always having to be so perfect...

Sometimes she must think the others don't really know her.

Who does she want to look so perfect for?

What if she weren't so beautiful?

Julia may not be as beautiful as Marlene,

but Tony would love to have her for a friend.

He told me so himself.

So far he's been to shy to tell her.

But maybe today he will…

Today seems to be the day
for making new friends.
Remember Max?
He went and hid out in the
schoolyard after break.
Paul was there too.
The two of them had a long talk.
It looks as though they've each
found a friend.
And as you know, you're stronger
when there are two of you...

So, now you know what it's like at our school.

What's it like at yours?

	Monday	Tuesd
	In respect to links in the book, the Publisher expressly notes that no illegal content was discernible on the linked sites at the time the links were created. The Publisher has no influence at all over the current and future design, content or authorship of the linked sites. For this reason the Publisher expressly disassociates itself from all content on linked sites that has been altered since the link was created and assumes no liability for such content.	
	Project management: Melanie Schöni Copyediting: John Son Production management: Susanne Hermann Typesetting: textum GmbH, Feldafing Printing and binding: DZS Grafik d.o.o.	

Project management: Melanie Schöni
Copyediting: John Son
Production management: Susanne Hermann
Typesetting: textum GmbH, Feldafing
Printing and binding: DZS Grafik d.o.o.